14 Days

NOV. 1 5 1988
AUG. 3 0 1989   JAN 8   1993
OCT. 5   1989   FEB 3   1993   JUL 1 9 2000
OCT. 9   1989   MAR 2 4 1993   SEP 2 8 2000
JAN 8   1990   MAY 1 7 1993
JAN. 2 4 1990   JUN   4 1993   1 2001
FEB. 2   1990   MAR   7 2001
MAR. 1 2 1990   JUL 2 9 1993   MAY 1 4 2001
JUN.   7 1990   FEB 1 0 1994   SEP   1 2001
JUN. 1 1 1990   FEB 1 6 2002
JUN. 2 6 1990   MAR 1 4 1994   OCT 1 4 2002
AUG. 1 3 1990   JUN   7 1994
OCT. 1 0 1990   MAY 3 0 1995   JUN 2 2 '06
OCT. 3 0 1990   JUN 2 6 1995   OCT 12 '06
DEC. 8   1990   JUL 2 1 1995   MAR 13 '07
                 AUG   4 1997   AUG 13 '07
JUL. 2 4 1991   OCT 2 5 1997   APR 0 8 2010
AUG. 2   1991   JAN 2 0 1998   AUG 0 1 2011
                 DEC   1 1998
AUG 3 1 1991   DEC 1 8 1998
JUN 1 0 1992   JUL 2 3 1999
SEP 2 1 1992   MAY   6 2000
                 JUN 2 6 2000

1991

WITHDRAWN

Raggedy Ann and Andy Go Flying

Raggedy Ann and Andy Go Flying

By Mary Fulton

Illustrated by Judith Hunt

BASED ON THE CHARACTERS CREATED BY JOHNNY GRUELLE

GOLDEN PRESS • NEW YORK
Western Publishing Company, Inc., Racine, Wisconsin

CDEFGHIJ

What excitement in the playroom — Marcella had been packing all morning. "I wish I could take you all with me," she told the dolls, hurrying to close her suitcase. "This is my first trip on an airplane. It's going to be such fun flying!"

Raggedy Ann and Andy were neatly tucked in their beds.
"Be good while I'm at Grandma's," Marcella told them,
"and take care of the other dolls for me. When I get back next
week, I'll tell you all about my flight."
Raggedy Ann and Andy just smiled, for dolls don't talk to people.

But as soon as Marcella slammed the front door, Raggedy Ann popped out of bed. "I wish I could go flying, too!" she cried.

"So do I!" shouted Raggedy Andy, jumping out of bed.

"*Ruff-ruff,*" barked Raggedy Arthur.

"I would love to zoom up
in a plane," said Ann.
"I would love to fly like
a bird," said Andy.

Suddenly Ann stopped pretending to fly, ran to
the window, and looked out. "I've got it!" she cried.
"We *can* go flying! Come on, Andy, follow me!"

Raggedy Andy and Raggedy
Arthur couldn't imagine what
Ann was thinking of.
But they followed
her as she raced
down the
stairs . . .

... out the door ...

... across the yard,
and down to the pond.

A big white goose was swimming in the pond.
Ann politely asked him if he would take them flying.

"No one can fly higher or faster than I can," boasted
the goose. "I'll be glad to take you."

"Hooray!" cried Ann and Andy together.

Raggedy Arthur just shook his head and growled.
He didn't want any part of flying.

"Let's go!" shouted Andy, and
he hopped aboard the goose's back.
    "Wait for me!" exclaimed
Raggedy Ann, grabbing Andy's hand.
    "Hold on tight!" honked the goose.
He took a few running steps,
flapped his wings, and
left the ground.

"*Ruff-ruff-ruff*," barked Raggedy Arthur frantically
as the goose soared into the sky, carrying his friends.

Raggedy Ann and Andy watched as Marcella's house got smaller and smaller. The pond became just a tiny patch of blue. Raggedy Arthur, a little speck of yellow, was running round and round in circles.

"Look, Andy," cried Ann. "Isn't it beautiful?"

"Whoopee!" yelled Andy. "We're flying! We're really flying!"

"Flying!" honked the goose. "You call this flying?" With that he raised one wing overhead and went into a dive.

"Oh, my goodness!" cried Andy, grabbing his hat.

"Oh!" gasped Ann as the pond got closer and closer.

Suddenly Ann found herself face to face with a fish.

But before she could even say hello, the goose was up and away again.

"Now you're really going to see something,"
said the goose, and he began to swoop and soar like
a roller-coaster. He had forgotten his passengers.
"Hang on, Ann!" shouted Andy.
"I'm trying, Andy," cried Raggedy Ann.

Suddenly the goose
turned a loop-the-loop and
Ann and Andy fell off.

"Help, help!" cried
Raggedy Ann, flapping her
arms as she fell toward the
ground.

Then her skirt billowed
up around her face and she
realized it was almost as
good as a parachute. She
looked around for Andy. He
was using his hat to catch
the wind and slow his fall.

"Oof," said Andy, thumping onto the ground.
"Whoof," said Ann, as she landed on something soft.
"*Ruff-ruff,*" said Raggedy Arthur, because he was
the something soft Raggedy Ann had landed on.

"It's a good thing we're made of cotton," said Ann
when she saw that Andy and Arthur were all right.

"Look at that," Ann said,
as Andy helped her up.
"We've landed in our yard."
"Good," said Andy.
"I certainly don't feel like
walking home after what
we've just been through."

Then, with wobbly knees, the three
Raggedys made their way back
to Marcella's playroom.

When Marcella came back from her trip,
the dolls were neatly tucked in their beds, just as she
had left them a week earlier.

"I'm so glad to be home," she said, hugging Ann and Andy.

"My goodness, you're all lumpy!" she exclaimed.
"How in the world did your stuffing get so bunched up?"

Raggedy Ann and Andy winked at each other secretly.
"Now," said Marcella, after she had patted
them back into shape, "let me tell you all
about flying. You've no *idea*
how exciting it can be!"